Su CLASS ....

AUTHOR.   FOREMAN, M.

BOOK NO.   Y 0380417

!

DATE OF RETURN

**WESTERN EDUCATION AND LIBRARY BOARD.
LIBRARY SERVICE.**

Books can be renewed, by personal application, post or telephone, quoting latest date, author and book number.

NO RENEWALS CAN BE GRANTED FOR A BOOK RESERVED BY ANOTHER READER.

Readers are expected to take care of books. L---
damaged books must be paid for by the borro---
concerned.
PD58

For John Salmon,
who really did surprise his mum.

A Red Fox Book

Published by Random House Children's Books
20 Vauxhall Bridge Road, London SW1V 2SA

A division of Random House UK Ltd
London Melbourne Sydney Auckland
Johannesburg and agencies throughout the world

Copyright © Michael Foreman 1995

1 3 5 7 9 10 8 6 4 2

First published in Great Britain by Andersen Press Ltd 1995

Red Fox edition 1999

Printed in Hong Kong

RANDOM HOUSE UK Limited Reg. No. 954009

ISBN 0 09 961091 4

Surprise! Surprise!

Written and illustrated by
Michael Foreman

Red Fox

Mum finished the story and kissed Little Panda goodnight.
Little Panda snuggled down in his bed and went to sleep
in the glow of his Moonlight.

He loved his Moonlight. It kept the dark away and Little Panda was frightened of the dark.

The next night it was Dad's turn to read. When he finished the story he kissed Little Panda goodnight. Then he said, "It's Mum's birthday soon. What will you give her for a present?" "A surprise," said Little Panda.

The next day, Little Panda
opened his piggy bank. He
found two chocolate buttons,
a bottle top and a shiny silver
coin. He sucked the chocolate
buttons while he wondered
what he could buy with a
bottle top and a
shiny silver
coin.

He went to the shop.
"May I have the biggest plant
I can get for this shiny silver
coin, please," said Little Panda.

The shopkeeper looked at
Little Panda's money and
gave him a tiny plant in a pot.
"It's very small," said Little Panda.
"So is your coin," said the
shopkeeper.

The plant was so tiny that Little Panda was able to take it home without his mum noticing.

Although he hated to go there, he hid it in the attic, as he knew it was the only place his mum wouldn't look.

Ooooh ... spooky! It was so dark.

Little Panda wanted to run
back downstairs, but he knew
he must be brave. He took a
deep breath and read the
label on the pot.
'This plant likes plenty of water
and sunlight.'

Little Panda gave the plant a
drink from the big water tank,
and then he had an idea . . .
he didn't know how to give the
plant sunlight, but he did have
his Moonlight.

That night, after Mum and Dad had kissed him goodnight, Little Panda crept out of bed and took his Moonlight to the attic.

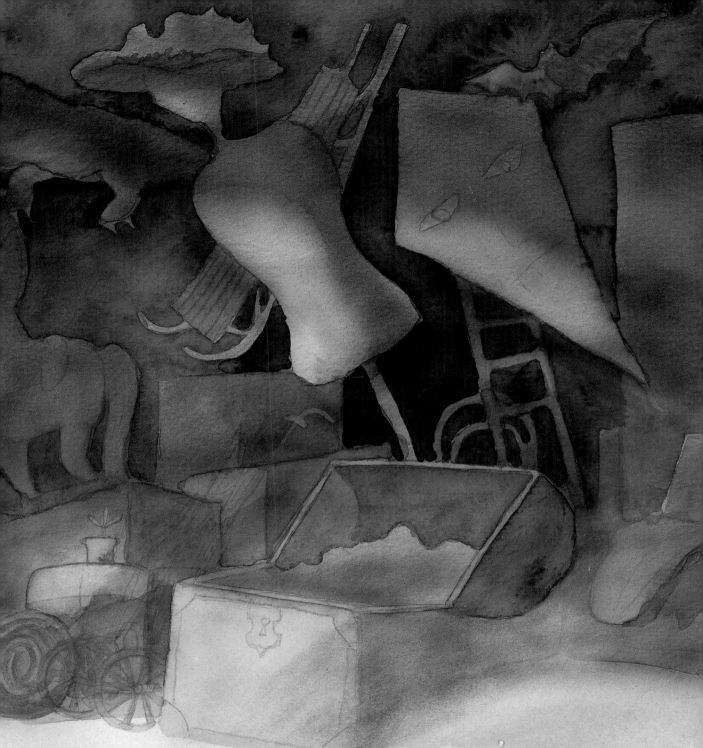

The attic was even more spooky at night than in the day. Little Panda thought the plant would be happier with his Moonlight.

Little Panda's room was now even darker than the attic, but he was brave. The tiny plant needed the Moonlight more than he did.

In the morning he got the Moonlight from the attic and put it back beside his bed before Mum called him for breakfast.

Every night, Little Panda gave the plant a drink and his Moonlight. Soon, he got used to the dark and didn't find it frightening any more.

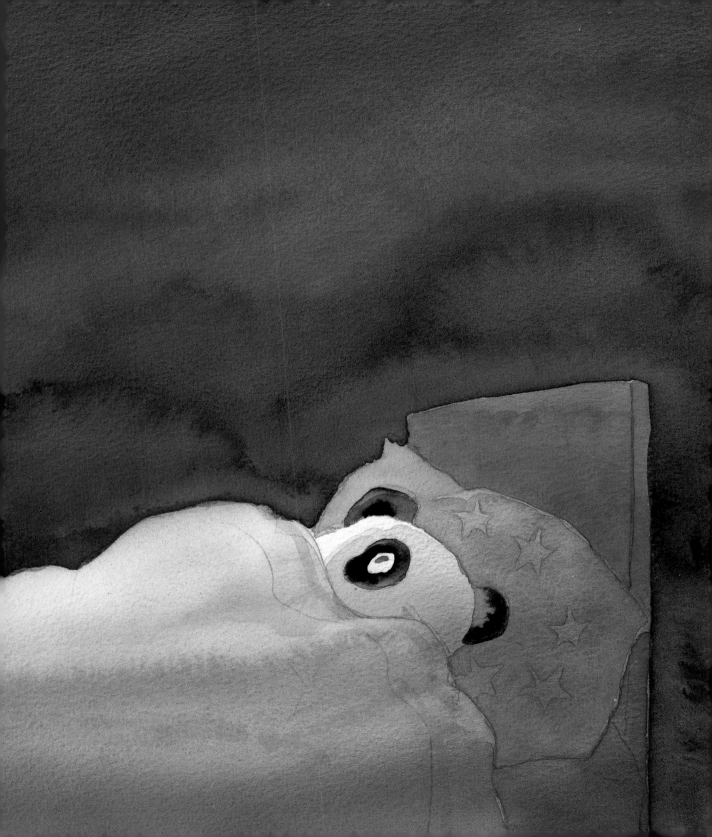

At last it was Mum's birthday.

Little Panda waited while
Mum had breakfast in bed.
He waited and waited while
Mum opened her present
from Dad. He waited and
waited and waited while
Mum opened all her birthday
cards.

Then Little Panda said, "Follow me!"
His mum and dad followed him upstairs,
and Little Panda opened the door to the attic!

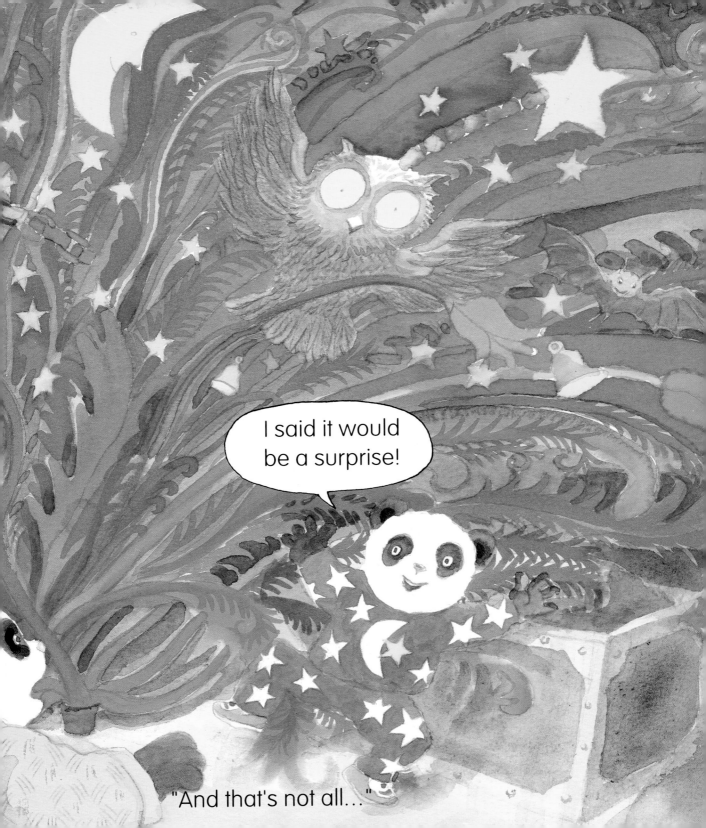